MW00900504

A Note for Parents

Many children grow up with impatient,
unloving, and abusive fathers, and
when someone says, "God is your loving
Father," they cannot relate. Hopefully,
this book will help children realize
what life with a loving father is like.

www.mascotbooks.com

The Ruth Adventures: Life on the Farm

©2020 Nancy Youngdahl. All Rights Reserved. No part of this publication may be reproduced, stored in a retrieval system or transmitted in any form by any means electronic, mechanical, or photocopying, recording or otherwise without the permission of the author.

For more information, please contact:
Mascot Books
620 Herndon Parkway, Suite 320
Herndon, VA 20170
info@mascotbooks.com

Library of Congress Control Number: 2019918393

CPSIA Code: PRT0120A
ISBN-13: 978-1-64543-105-3

Printed in the United States

THE RUTH ADVENTURES

LIFE ON THE FARM

Nancy
Youngdahl

illustrated by
Diana Delosh

My name is Ruth and I'm six years old. I live on a big farm in North Carolina with my mama, daddy, and big brother, Samuel. Every morning Daddy greets me with a big hug, and words like "Give me some sugar," which means, "I love you and I want a kiss!"

Daddy is always calling me "sweetie" and saying I'm his baby girl. That makes me feel very special. I know he loves me because when I'm angry or upset, he gently corrects me with words full of encouragement, like "Now little girl, don't you fret! Everything will be okay."

I told Mama that when I grow up, I'm gonna marry someone just like my daddy! Daddy and I are the best of friends.

Daddy told me I can be a farmer like him when I grow up, if I want to. Helping around the farm with Daddy is fun. He loves showing me how to plant the corn and wheat that we grow. Daddy lets me sit on his lap to drive the big tractor. He says I am a quick learner!

I also like to watch my brother Samuel clean out the horse stalls and put down clean straw. Someday I'll be able to do that!

I get to help feed all the animals that live in our barn: chickens, rabbits, ducks, horses, and best of all, puppies and kittens. Our mama cat, Fluffy, always has kittens for me to play with. Mama likes to have a lot of cats living in the barn since they keep the mice away. Mama and I don't like mice!

Daddy works very hard in the fields all day long, but at nighttime he takes time to read me one of my favorite stories before I go to sleep. Daddy and Mama teach me my prayers and tell me that my other Father, God, loves me even more than they do! They always make sure I am tucked in and kiss me goodnight. If Daddy is plumb tuckered out from all his work or is still out in the barn, Mama will read to me and help me with my prayers.

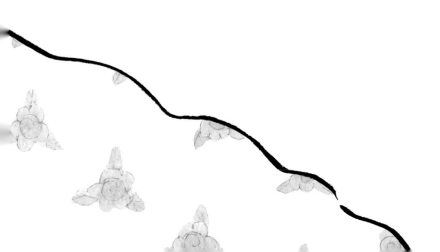

Daddy doesn't work on Sundays, so after church I invite him to a tea party. He even knows how to hold the teacup with his little finger pointed up! Daddy and I always dress up in our "Sunday best clothes" so we can look fancy. I wear make-believe grown-up clothes that Aunt Beatrice gave me for playtime.

Daddy always wears a necktie and takes special care to have his hair combed nice. We always invite my doll, Margaret, and my stuffed rabbit, Harry, to join us for tea. They dress up fancy too. Daddy looks very funny sitting in a little chair around my small table with his knees way up in the air!

We laugh a lot and share stories about our week. I told Daddy that Harry and I played in a puddle of water this week and got all dirty. Harry looked so funny when his fur got all muddy and his ears were flopping down and dripping with water.

Mama put Harry in the washing machine and then out in the sun to dry before he could join us for tea. This story made Daddy laugh!

Mama fixes my "ouches" when I get hurt. If Daddy is around, he will hold me tight until I stop crying. Once, Mama got "madder than a wet hen" when our old donkey, Ralph, bit me with its big teeth.

She told Daddy and he tied that
old donkey up in the barn instead
of letting him run free in the field!

It was probably my fault though, since I was trying to take an apple away from Ralph as he was snacking on apples under the shade of our old apple tree.

That night at bedtime, I confessed to Daddy what I had done to cause Ralph to bite me. I felt better in my heart since I told Daddy the truth and because Daddy promised to let Ralph go back in the field the next morning. I knew that would make Ralph happy! When I went out to do my chores the next day, I smiled big when I saw Ralph back in the field and under the old apple tree.

Summer is my favorite time of the year since I get to play outside all day when it's not raining and I don't have to go to school. Mama even lets me go barefoot when I'm not doing my chores or running around in the barn or helping my daddy and brother, Samuel, in the field. I like the feel of dirt and mud between my toes!

In the winter evenings when it's cold and snowy outside, I like to snuggle up close to Daddy when he's in his big chair in front of the warm fire.

That's a very special time for me because I feel so safe and loved and can go to sleep knowing in the morning I will be in my own bed when I wake up. I know I'll have another happy day with my family and all the animals I help take care of.

Right after breakfast I put on my coveralls, boots, and coat and run out to the barn so I can do my chores before I do my schoolwork.

The animals are always waiting for me to feed them! Growing up in a home where you are loved is the best thing in the whole world!

ABOUT THE AUTHOR

This is Nancy's third children's book. Nancy and her husband, Skip, live in Mebane, North Carolina, and enjoy their "senior years" as parents, grandparents, and even great-grandparents. Nancy enjoys reading, writing, golf, watercolor painting, traveling, visiting family, church fellowship, spending time with neighbors, and being lazy when time permits. Look for Nancy's other children's books, *My Nana Was A Free-Range Kid*, *Remembering Joseph Chickadee*, and her upcoming fourth book, featuring another adventure with Ruth. Nancy would enjoy hearing from you. Her email address is nancy.p.youngdahl@gmail.com.